Step back in time to the adventurous saga of the settling of the Plymouth Colony, including the first Thanksgiving.

"This book will be a welcomed addition to libraries."
—*Booklist*

". . .a fine text by Robert San Souci; and superlative production."
—*Horn Book*

"What makes this book special is that it is to be experienced as a healthy fairy tale told with artistic potency and a strong sense of the human scale of history"
—*School Library Journal*

"A copy of this book should be in every school."
—*The Midwest Review of Books*

The names of those which came ouer first, in ye year 1620.
and were (by the blesing of god) the first begiñers, and
(in a sort) the foundation, of all the plantations, and
Colonies, in New-England (and their families)

8 m John Caruer.
kathrine his wife.
Desire minter; &
2. man-seruants
John Howland
Roger Wilder.
William Latham, a boy.
& a maid seruant; & a
child yt was put to him
called, Jasper More

m William Brewster.
Mary his wife, with
6 2 sons, whose names
were Loue, & Wrasling.
and a boy was put to
him called Richard More; and another
of his brothers
the rest of his Childeren
were left behind & came
ouer afterwards.

m Edward Winslow
Elizabeth his wife, &
5 2 men seruants, caled
Georg Sowle, and
Elias Story; also a litle
girle was put to him caled
Ellen, the sister of Richard
More.

2 William Bradford, and
Dorathy his wife, hauing
but one Child, a sone left
behind, who came afterward.

m Isaack Allerton, and
6 Mary his wife; with 3. Children
Bartholmew
Remember, &
Mary. and a seruant boy,
John Hooke.

2 Captin Myles Standish
and Rose, his wife

4 m Christopher Martin,
and his wife; and 2. seruants,
Salamon prower, and
John Langemore

5 m William Mullines, and his
wife; and 2. Children
Joseph, & priscila; and a seruant
Robart Carter.

6 m white William White, and
Susana his wife; and one sone
Caled resolued, and one borne
a ship-bord caled perigriene; &
2. seruants, named
William Holbeck, & Edward Thomson

8 m Hopins Steuen Hopkins, &
Elizabeth his wife; and 2.
Children, caled giles, and
Constanta a doughter, both
by a former wife. And 2. more
by this wife, caled Damaris, &
Oceanus, the last was borne at
Sea. And 2. seruants, called
Edward Doty, and Edward Litster.

1 m Richard Warren, but his
wife and Children were lefte
behind and came afterwards

4 John Billinton, and Elen his wife:
and 2. sones John, & francis.

4 Edward Tillie, and ann his wife:

2 Francis Cooke, and his sone John;
But his wife & other Children came
afterwards

2 Thomas Rogers, and Joseph his
sone; his other Children came after
wards

2 Thomas Tinker, and his wife, and a
sone

2 John Rigdale; and slice his
wife.

3 James Chilton, and his wife, and
Mary their doughter; they had an
other doughter yt was maried came
aftermart.

3 Edward fuller, and his wife; and
Samuell their sonne.

3 John Turner, and 2. sones; he
had a doughter came some years
after to Salem, wher she is now
liuing.

3 Francis Eaton. and Sarah his
wife, and samuell their sone, a yong
Child

Moyses fletcher
John Goodman
Thomas Williams
10 Digerie preist
Edmond Wargeson
Peter Browne
Richard Britterige
Richard Clarke
Richard Gardenar
Gilbart Winslow

John Alden was hired for a
Cooper, at South-Hampton wher
1 the ship victuled; and being
a hopfull yongman was

And ther 2 dougter, one, all liuing and other of their children marigable. so 15 are come of them.

mr Brewster liued to very old age; about 80 years, he was when he dyed, hauing liued some 23 or 24 years here in ye countrie. And though his wife dyed long before, yet she dyed aged. His sone was tho dyed a yonge man vnmaried; his sone Loue, till this year 1650 and dyed, & left 4 children, now liuing. His doughters which came ouer after him, are dead but haue left sundry children aliue; his eldst sone is still liueing, and hath 9 or 10 children, one maried who hath a child, or 2.
Richard more, his Brother dyed the first winter; but he is maried, and hath 4 or 5 children, all liuing.

mr Ed: Winslow, his wife dyed the first winter; and he maried with the widow of mr White, and hath 2 children liuing by her marigable, besids sundry that are dead: one of his seruants dyed, as also the litle girls soone after the ships ariuall. But his man Georg Sowle is still liuing, and hath 8 childrē

William Bradford, his wife dyed soone after their ariuall; and he maried againe; and hath 4 children, 3 wherof are maried. 7
who dyed 9 of May 1655.

mr Allerton his wife dyed with the first, and his seruant John Hooke, his sone Bartle is maried in England but I know not how many children he hath. His doughter remember is . . .

mr fuller, his seruant dyed at sea; and after his wife came ouer, he had tow children by her; which are liuing and growne up to yers. But he dyed some 15 years agoe. 2

John Crakston dyed in the first mortality; and about some 5 or 6 years after his sone dyed, hauing lost him selfe in ye wodes, his feet became frosen, which put him into a feauor, of which he dyed. 6

Captain Standish his wife dyed in the first sicknes; and he maried againe, and hath 4 sones liue: ing, and some are dead. 4
— who dyed 3 of octob: 1656.

mr Martin, he and all his, dyed in the first Infection; not long after the ariuall.

mr Molines, and his wife, his sone, & his seruant dyed the first winter. Only his dougter Priscila suruied, and maried with John Alden, who are both liuing, and haue 11 children. And their eldest daughter is maried & hath fiue children. See N. E. Memorial. p. 22. 15

mr White, and his 2 seruants dyed soone after ther landing. His wife maried with mr Winslow (as is before noted) His 2 sons are maried, and resolued hath 5 children; perigrine tow, all liuing: so their Increase are 7. 7

mr Hopkins, and his wife are now both dead. But they liued aboue . . .

his doughter Constanta, is also maried. and hath 12 children all of them liuing, and one of them maried 12

mr Richard Warren liued some 4 or 5 years, and had his wife come ouer to him, by whom he had 2 sons before dyed; and one of them is maryed, and hath 2 children so his yncrease is 4. But he had 5 doughters more came ouer with his wife, who are all maried, & liuing & haue many children. 4

John Billinton after he had bene here 10 yers, was executed, for killing a man; and his eldest sone dyed before him; But his 2 sone is aliue, and maried & hath 8 children 8

Edward Tillie, and his wife both dyed soone after their ariuall; and the girle Humility their cousen was sent for into Ento England, and dyed ther. But the youth Henery samson, is still liueing, and is maried, & hath 7 children. 7

John Tillie, and his wife both dyed, alitle after they came a shore; and their daughter Elizabeth maried with John Howland and hath yssue as is before noted.

francis Cooke is . . .

N.C.WYETH'S PILGRIMS

To the Schoolteachers of America —
Those friends I have met or have yet to meet
Who every day keep the Pilgrims' dream alive,
In classrooms from Plymouth to Pago Pago.

The author and editor wish to extend special thanks to the Plimouth Plantation for their enthusiastic and invaluable guidance in the preparation of the text for this book, and to the Metropolitan Life Insurance Company, especially Mr. Stephen Loesch, for their gracious and generous help in making this book possible.

Illustrations courtesy of Metropolitan Life Insurance Company
Photographer: Malcom Varon
Text copyright ©1991 by Robert San Souci.
Illustrations copyright ©1945 by Metropolitan Life Insurance Company
All rights reserved.

The endpapers of this book are copies of the Mayflower's original passenger list, courtesy of the Plimouth Plantation.
Book design by Kathy Warinner.
Typeset in Weiss.

10 9 8 7 6 5

Chronicle Books
85 Second Street
San Francisco, California 94105

www.chroniclekids.com

Library of Congress Cataloging-in-Publication Data

San Souci, Robert D.
    N. C. Wyeth's pilgrims / by Robert San Souci
        p.   cm.
    Summary: Recounts the coming of the Pilgrims to America, with illustrations by N. C. Wyeth.
    ISBN: 0-8118-1486-6 (pb)   0-87701-806-5 (hc)
    1. Pilgrims (New Plymouth Colony)--Juvenile literature.
2. Pilgrims (New Plymouth Colony) in art--Juvenile literature.
3. Massachusetts--History--New Plymouth, 1620-1691--Juvenile literature. [1. Pilgrims (New Plymouth Colony) 2. Pilgrims (New Plymouth Colony) in art. 3. Massachusetts--History--New Plymouth, 1620-1691.] I. Wyeth, N. C. (Newell Convers), 1882-1945, ill. II. Title.
F68.S2 1991
974.4'82--dc20

Distributed in Canada by Raincoast Books
8680 Cambie Street, Vancouver, B.C. V6P 6M9

Manufactured in China.

N.C. WYETH'S PILGRIMS

TEXT BY ROBERT SAN SOUCI

CHRONICLE BOOKS ❦ SAN FRANCISCO

he sixteenth and seventeenth centuries were a time of religious struggle in England. The rulers wanted their subjects to follow the established church, but some people held different beliefs. One such group, referred to as "Separatists," held secret meetings, but they grew afraid when some of their members were put in prison. They left England for Holland, but they could not settle comfortably among the Dutch. As time passed, they heard stories of a settlement in North America called Virginia. This New World promised land, economic opportunity and, most importantly, the hope of religious freedom. So the Separatists decided to cross the ocean and establish a colony of their own.

They made an agreement with a group of London businessmen: the settlers would receive passage and supplies and in return, they would send the London Company fish, fur, and lumber for seven years. The Separatists in Holland bought a ship, the *Speedwell*. Those in London hired another ship, the *Mayflower*. Even with two ships, many of the Separatists were left behind with the hope of making the crossing later.

Both ships set sail from Southampton, England, but twice the leaky *Speedwell* had to turn back. Each time the *Mayflower* followed her, and finally, on September 6, 1620, the *Mayflower* alone departed from Plymouth, England on her historic voyage.

hile no pictures survive, researchers have reconstructed the *Mayflower's* appearance from documents and paintings of the time. Likely, she was a three-masted ship, ninety feet long, with a crew of twenty-five sailors.

Of the one hundred and two passengers crowded into the damp quarters, forty-four (nineteen men, eleven women, and fourteen children) were Separatists. The others had been recruited by the London Company. Referred to by the Separatists as "Strangers," they did not entirely share the Separatists' religious beliefs, but they did share a desire for a new life in a new land. These included Myles Standish, a professional soldier hired as the commander of the Separatists' militia. There were also some hens, goats, and two dogs.

Noise was a constant companion: timbers creaked; sails and rigging flapped; rats scratched; and bilge water gurgled. At night, some ninety people slept in the area known as "tween decks"– most on straw mattresses on the hard floor. The stuffy space was also cluttered with chests, barrels of provisions, and building equipment. There was not a place on board where there was silence or solitude.

The overcrowding taxed everyone, and tensions ran high between the passengers and the sailors. The crew resented the Separatists' daily Psalm-singing and prayers, while the Pilgrims disliked the sailors' swearing. The pitch and roll of rough waves made seasickness a constant problem. For those passengers not too seasick to eat, most meals were simple: salted meat or fish and hard, dry ship's biscuit. There were also dried peas and beans, dried fruits, cheese, and butter. The food was washed down with beer, which even the children drank. Lice, boredom, homesickness, and fear added to the misery. During the journey, a servant to the group's doctor died of a fever and was buried at sea. A boy was born and named "Oceanus."

The weather ranged from fair and gentle to raging storms. During one storm, the ship's main beam cracked. Some thought all was lost, but the ship rode out the storm, and the beam was repaired with an iron screw that had been brought for house-building. In the course of another storm, a passenger fell overboard, but managed to catch hold of a rope that was trailing in the water and was hauled back to safety.

So it was a weary group that heard the first cries of "Land ho!" and crowded the railing for a look at their new home. For sixty-six days they had been at sea, but on November 11, 1620, their adventurous journey ended – or so they thought. In fact, many more adventures and dangers lay ahead.

From the deck of the ship, the passengers gazed at a bleak landscape. Some of the sailors muttered that the place was filled with wild beasts and wild men, called "Indians." A few of the passengers talked of returning to England, but most were determined to stay and soon began to discuss what to do next.

Because they had landed so far from their intended goal, Virginia, the Strangers felt that they should not have to honor their agreement with the London merchants. But the Separatists argued that they should proceed as they had planned. Ultimately, the Strangers agreed, and together the two groups drafted an agreement, known as the "Mayflower Compact," which set out the principles that would govern their settlement. From this point, the groups became so intermingled that all have become known as "Pilgrims."

he first exploring party left the ship on November 11th. They replenished their dwindling supplies of wood and water, and marveled at the abundance to be found in their new homeland. On Monday, November, 13th, a landing was made to repair the shallop (a small boat used for exploring). While the men repaired, the women washed clothes. Since there had been little chance to do more than rinse in salt water on the *Mayflower,* the washing took all day. Spread out to air that first washday was a rainbow of clothes: red skirts, blue pants, purple capes, and green stockings.

Soon after, a second scouting party went out. On this trip, they found the remains of a hut with curious mounds nearby. Digging into the mounds, the explorers found baskets filled with corn. They named this place "Corn Hill" and brought forty bushels of corn back to the ship, promising themselves to make payment later (which they eventually did). To the Pilgrims aboard the *Mayflower,* the strange, multi-colored corn must have seemed a fortunate sign indeed. With enough seed corn to plant in the spring, they now felt more hopeful about their prospects.

But winter winds and icy rain soon drove all but the hardiest sailors below deck. Men returning from runs to shore reported the ground was covered with snow. The need to find a place for their colony grew more urgent than ever. For many, the situation must have seemed little better than when they were on the high seas. They wondered if they were ever going to find the right spot to build their new home.

Many more scouting parties went out, including one that ventured out in the shallop in mid-December. One night during this trip, while camped on shore, they heard a strange cry. Frightened and confused, the men fired their muskets in all directions, and the noise stopped. They assured themselves that they had heard only the cry of wolves, but sleep did not come easily.

Early the next morning, they heard the cry again. The Pilgrims retreated, firing two shots. The Indians, still at a distance, continued their cries. They shot a few arrows at the Pilgrims and then fled.

Though the barricade bristled with arrows, miraculously no one, Indian or Pilgrim, had been wounded.

The Pilgrims gathered the arrows – which were eventually sent back to England as "curiosities"– and continued their explorations. They named the site "First Encounter."

On Friday, December 9, the Pilgrims discovered a small cove. The following Monday, they sounded the waters and found them deep enough to harbor large ships. Then they moored the shallop and explored inland, where they found some abandoned corn fields, forests that would provide timber, and a number of freshwater streams. Here was the site they had been seeking.

he Pilgrims spent much of their first winter living aboard the *Mayflower*. They had only two small boats, and winter weather slowed the unloading process even more. As some unloaded the ship, others began work on a few small cabins as well as a common house, where most would live and where goods could be stored. A fire that destroyed the thatched roof of the common house slowed the work even further. In that desolate place, not a scrap could afford to be lost, so everyone worked frantically to salvage the stored goods. While most of what was stored inside was saved, repairs could not be made because illness had begun to take a terrible toll.

Deadliest of all was pneumonia (though at the time, the Pilgrims believed that it was scurvy), caused by poor shelter and by the constant wading in winter's cold waters to get from shallop to shore. By April, half the Pilgrims had died – sometimes as many as two or three in a single day. A handful of people, including Captain Myles Standish, remained healthy. But in spite of their tireless efforts, the deaths continued. Because of their dwindling numbers, the Pilgrims began to fear attacks by the Indians.

But the Indians remained at a distance. Once they took some unguarded tools, but they would run off if approached by a Pilgrim.

Toward the middle of March, however, an Indian warrior strode boldly into Plymouth. He spoke a curious English that was hard for the Pilgrims to understand, but they learned his name was Samoset. He was an Abnaki sagamore, or chief, from what is now Maine, and he came on behalf of a tribe called the Pokanoket (now called the Wampanoag). He spoke of another Indian named Squanto who had actually been to England.

The Pilgrims fed Samoset and sent him on his way with gifts. He soon returned with five me

nd the stolen tools. He announced that a great chief, Massasoit, was coming to visit the colony.

he chief arrived several days later with a number of warriors, including Squanto. Food was shared, gifts were presented to the Indians, and a peace treaty was forged that endured for many years. When the Indians departed, Squanto stayed behind to act as an interpreter.

Squanto revealed that when he returned to North America after his first journey to London, he had been kidnapped by a ship's captain who planned to sell him as a slave. But Squanto escaped back to England. Eventually he was brought to New England, but he found that his tribe, the Patuxet, had been wiped out by disease. He was the sole survivor.

To the struggling community, Squanto proved to be far more than an interpreter. He taught the Pilgrims how to harvest the natural bounty of the woods, where the best fishing waters were, and how to plant corn using fish as fertilizer. He served as a guide and as a go-between in buying furs from the Indians. Squanto remained at Plymouth until his death, in 1622.

On April 5, 1621, the *Mayflower* returned to England. With the ship gone, the Pilgrims would be wholly dependent on the land and the work of their own hands until the arrival of the next ship. The ship's captain offered to take anyone who wanted to return to England, but not a single Pilgrim accepted his offer.

That first spring, Governor John Carver died, yet, for most the warming weather brought general health and a sense of relief. Though they had lost half their company, the Plymouth Colony was surviving.

Everywhere there were the sights and sounds of activity. The Pilgrims applied old skills and quickly learned new ones. Boys watched over the fields, hunted, made wooden pegs to fasten beams, and helped build houses. Both boys and girls gathered mussels and clams, turned spits for roasting, and stuffed linen sacks with leaves, corn husks or feathers to make mattresses. When time permitted, the children learned their ABCs and practiced their reading by studying the Bible and psalter songbooks.

More and more life took on a settled aspect. There were romances and weddings, birth

d deaths. The colony was beginning to be caught in the rhythm of village life.

**T**he sea yielded a bounty of fish and there were signs that the harvest would be good enough to get them through the coming winter. Even at the height of summer, the Pilgrims had begun preparing for the winter that lay ahead. Corn was shucked and stored away. Fruits were dried and vegetables were pickled. Fish were dried and packed in salt, while meats were cured over smokey fires. In celebration of this plenty, plans were made to hold a Harvest Festival. This feast, that we have come to call "Thanksgiving," would also celebrate the help the Indians had given the Pilgrims.

The food was plentiful. Though the barley and peas (from seeds brought from England) had done poorly, they had their fill of beans, corn, and squash. There was cod and sea bass which were grilled or served in stews, along with eels, lobsters, mussels, and clams.

There was pumpkin pudding and skillet breads of corn meal, as well as wild grapes and crab apples, dried strawberries and gooseberries. To supplement the harvest, the colony's new governor, William Bradford, sent some men to hunt ducks, geese, and wild turkeys.

For three days, the Pilgrims feasted. The children played games. The men had contests to test their skill with a musket. At the height of the festivities, Chief Massasoit arrived with

ninety men, women, and children. A few of the men left briefly and returned with five deer which were added to the feast. All the while, the colony was filled with chatter and laughter.

his first "Thanksgiving" reminded the Pilgrims of all they had to be thankful for and made them confident that their settlement would endure. Their Indian guests left with pledges of friendship and peace — a peace that lasted many years, until the growth of the colonies created tensions between the two groups.

The winter that followed was harsh, but not as difficult as the first winter had been. Another ship arrived bringing pigs, as well as a few new settlers who had no supplies of their own. But hard work and a willingness to share brought everyone through the winter. When spring came, it was clearer than ever that the Plymouth Colony would indeed endure.

In the days that followed, ships arriving from England brought necessities such as clothes, shoes, tools, and muskets as well as cloth, knives, beads, rugs, and trinkets to trade with the Indians. Small luxuries such as sugar, cheese, and spices also arrived. Later, cattle were sent. In return, the Pilgrims sent back cargoes of lumber, salt fish, and corn.

The adventure begun by a small group of brave men and women had developed into something greater than any of them could have imagined. The Pilgrims had weathered illness, privation, and danger of every kind. Plymouth Colony had taken root. In time, its children would become known as New Englanders and Americans and the seedling colony would blossom and bear extraordinary fruit.

AUTHOR'S NOTE

While writing this book, I consulted numerous sources, including William Bradford's account *Of Plymouth Plantation 1620-1647*, and his journal, which is among the documents incorporated in *Mourt's Relation* (1622), also by William Bradford (who succeeded John Carver as governor) and Edward Winslow (the first assistant governor and later governor as well). Visits to Plymouth, the *Mayflower II*, and the reconstructed Plimouth Plantation also provided important insights.

Some details of N.C. Wyeth's paintings differ from the reality of early Plymouth days. The Pilgrims did not wear somber clothing and starched white caps and collars every day; the furnishings of the cottage scene probably reflect a later period in the colony's history, cattle were not brought to Plymouth until 1624.

Spelling in the old texts sometimes varies so that "Plymouth" is also written "Plimouth," and "Myles" Standish, "Miles." The Pilgrims used a calendar that set dates earlier than today's calendars. This book uses the colony's original reckoning of dates.

As for the first "Thanksgiving," the Pilgrims' three-day feast reflects the Separatists' tradition of religious thanksgivings (though these were usually solemn affairs held in church). It also echoes Roman, Greek, and ancient Hebrew harvest festivals, Dutch "fast-prayer and thank days," and the annual English "Harvest Home" celebration.

In early America, religious thanksgivings were proclaimed by colonial councils or the fledgling Federal government as onetime events, usually in a particular community or region.

In 1777, the Continental Congress proclaimed the first national Thanksgiving – a day of quiet reflection – in honor of the defeat of the British at Saratoga. Later, Presidents George Washington, John Adams, and James Monroe also proclaimed national Thanksgivings, but by 1815, the custom had nearly died.

In 1827, Sarah Josepha Hale, a writer, began her nearly forty-year campaign to reinstate the holiday. On November 26, 1863, President Abraham Lincoln proclaimed an annual national Thanksgiving Day to be celebrated on the last Thursday in November. In 1939, President Franklin Delano Roosevelt moved Thanksgiving from the fourth to the third Thursday in November, but people were unhappy with the change. In 1941, a joint resolution of Congress reestablished the holiday on the fourth Thursday of November.

Today, Thanksgiving invites us to recall the Pilgrims' achievements and the original peace and friendship between Native Americans and the early settlers. This should encourage us to strive for a national harmony that reflects the ideals of those first Plymouth Days.

Robert D. San Souci

ABOUT THE ARTIST

Born in 1882, in Needham, Massachusetts, Newell Convers Wyeth was the first of three generations of an extraordinary family of artists. Influenced by his family's roots in the United States, his admiration for the work of Henry David Thoreau, and his studies under Howard Pyle (widely regarded as the father of American illustration), N.C. Wyeth was the consummate American artist.

In 1902, Wyeth traveled to Delaware, to study at Pyle's small school. His work quickly matured, and his first published illustration appeared on the cover of *The Saturday Evening Post* in 1903. The subject was a bronco buster and Wyeth was soon regarded as an illustrator of the American West.

Wyeth's most famous illustrations, however, were for children's classics, such as *Treasure Island*, *Robin Hood*, *The Last of the Mohicans*, and *Rip Van Winkle*. These volumes are now prized by collectors. Less known are Wyeth's murals which he painted for a wide variety of clients.

In 1940, Wyeth was asked to create a series of murals for the Metropolitan Life Insurance Company in New York. He proposed a historical series called "The Ballad of America" that would begin with the Pilgrims and continue through the California gold rush. Metropolitan Life decided to limit the series to the Plymouth Colony.In these murals, Wyeth challenged the existing notions of Pilgrim society as unremittingly severe by depicting the pleasures and beauty of the colony. The paintings reveal the romantic vision and lyricism that were the hallmarks of Wyeth's style.

The first two murals were installed in 1941. During the next four years, Wyeth expanded his original concept to include wildlife scenes of birds and deer in order to convey the bucolic peace he believed the Pilgrims found at Plymouth.

Wyeth was to finish fourteen of the murals, but before he could complete the rest, he died in an automobile accident on October 19, 1945.

In 1984, John Creedon, president and chief executive officer of Metropolitan Life approved a plan to clean and restore the murals. Margaret Watherston, a leading conservator of paintings, was retained to restore them, and today they are on permanent display.

The Metropolitan Life Murals were Wyeth's most extensive undertaking, and they embody the breadth of his artistic vision. In them can be found his deep emotional attachment to the natural world, to adventure and history, to America and all her peoples, and his own insistently positive view of the human experience.

The names of those which came over first, in yᵉ year ·1620·
and were (by the blesing of god) the first beginers, and
(in a sort) the foundation, of all the plantations, and
Colonies, in New-England (And their families·)

mʳ John Caruer.
kathrine his wife·
Desire minter; &
·2· man-servants
John Howland
Roger Wilder·
William Latham, a boy,
& a maid servant, & a
Child yᵗ was put to him
called, Jasper More

mʳ William Brewster.
Mary his wife, with
·2· sons, whose names
were Loue, & Wrasling·
and a boy was put to
him called Richard more; and another
of his Brothers
the rest of his Children
were left behind & came
ouer afterwards·

mʳ Edward Winslow
Elizabeth his wife, &
2 men servants, caled
Georg Sowle, and
Elias Story; also a litle
girle was put to him caled
Ellen, the sister of Richard
More·

William Bradford, and
Dorathy his wife, hauing
but one Child, a sone Left
behind, who came afterward·

mʳ Isaack Allerton, and
Mary·his wife; with ·3· Children
Bartholmew
Remember, &
Mary· and a servant boy,
John Hooke·

_Captin myles Standish
and Rose, his wife_ · 2·

mʳ Christopher martin,
and his wife; and ·2· servants,
Salamon prower, and
John Langemore · 4·

mʳ William mullines, and his
wife; and ·2· Children
Joseph, & priscila; and a servant
Robart Carter· · 5·

mʳ William White, and
Susana his wife; and one sone
Caled resolued, and one borne
· a ship-bord caled perigriene; &
·2· servants, named
William Holbeck, & Edward Thomson · 6·

mʳ Steuen Hopkins, &
Elizabeth his wife; and ·2·
Children, caled Giles, and
Constanta a doughter, both
by a former wife· And ·2· more
by this wife, caled Damaris, &
- oceanus, the last was borne at
Sea· And ·2· servants, called
Edward Doty, and Edward Litster· · 8·

mʳ Richard Warren, but his
wife and Children were Lefte
behind and came afterwards · 1·

John Billinton, and Elen his wife:
and ·2· sones John, & francis· · 4·

Edward Tillie, and Ann his wife: · 4·

Francis Cooke, and his sone John;
But his wife & other Children came
afterwards · 2·

Thomas Rogers, and Joseph his
sone; his other Children came after
wards· · 2·

Thomas Tinker, and his wife, and a
sone · 2·

John Rigdale; and Alice his
wife· · 2·

James Chilton, and his wife, and
Mary their dougter; they had an
other doughter yᵗ was maried came
afterwark· · 3·

Edward fuller, and his wife; and
Samuell their sonne· · 3·

John Turner, and ·2· sones; he
had a doughter came some years
after to Salem, wher she is now
liuing. · 3·

Francis Eaton. and Sarah his
wife, and Samuell their sone, a yong
Child · 3·

Moyses fletcher
John Goodman
Thomas Williams
Digorie preist
Edmond margeson
peter Browne
Richard Britterige
Richard Clarke
Richard Gardenar
Gilbart Winslow · 10·

John Alden was hired for a
Cooper, at South-Hampton wher
the ship Victuled; and being
a hopfull yongman was much